For Joshua

Library of Congress Cataloging-in-Publication Data
Nightingale, Sandy.
Cat's knees & bee's whiskers/
written and illustrated by Sandy Nightingale. — 1st U.S. ed.
p.   cm.
Summary: Baldrick the cat studies hard
to become an expert witch's cat, but he runs into trouble
when he tries out a new spell without supervision.
ISBN 0-15-215364-0
[1. Cats — Fiction. 2. Witches — Fiction.]
I. Title. II. Title: Cat's knees and bee's whiskers.
PZ7.N583Cat   1993
[E] — dc20   92-39811

Printed in Italy

A B C D E

CAT'S KNEES & BEE'S WHISKERS

Sandy Nightingale

HBJ

Harcourt Brace Jovanovich, Publishers

San Diego   New York   London

Printed in Italy

Baldrick was a witch's cat.

Well, to be absolutely truthful, he was only a beginner. He had a lot to learn.

He had answered an advertisement in *Witch* magazine. It read:

WANTED
Apprentice Witch's Cat.
Must be bright and have a good
head for heights.
No previous experience necessary.
Full training given.
Basket and Board.
Apply: Lobelia Gnomeclencher, Witch, 1st class

To Baldrick's surprise he got the job.

The first thing he had to learn was how to ride a broomstick.

It wasn't easy.

Everybody knows that a witch's cat must be able to loop the loop and do an emergency stop without turning a whisker.

Some of the other cats were very good. Baldrick thought he'd never get the hang of it.

But the most important part of his training was helping Lobelia with all her magic potions. To be a real witch's cat he had to pass the Silver Cauldron exam in spells and incantations. Baldrick studied late into the night for his diploma and Silver Cauldron Medal.

On top of this he had to do all the housework and cooking, and
Lobelia often invited her friends to tea. They all agreed that Baldrick
baked the lightest spongecake, the most scrumptious scones, and as for
his sugar-frosted mice . . . ah, mice!

If there was one thing Baldrick loved
more than anything else, it was mice . . .
Stalking mice. Chasing mice. Catching mice!
Very soon there were no mice left in Lobelia's house.

One afternoon, Lobelia had a very important visitor.
The great wizard Grimley Beamish came to ask a favor.

"I need a piece of green cheese to
finish a very clever spell," he explained
grandly. "And I trust no one but you
to get it for me."
Lobelia was very flattered.
"Leave it to me," she said.
"Where is it?"
"Why, Lobelia," replied the wizard
with a horrible smirk. "Everyone knows
that the moon is made of green cheese."

Baldrick couldn't believe his ears.
The moon made of cheese? he thought.
Everyone knows that where there's cheese
there's mice!

Lobelia began a moon spell at once. Her broomstick was rather old and worn and she was worried that it wouldn't manage to carry both her and Baldrick on such a long journey. So she planned to send it on its own. It would gather the green cheese like a giant bumble bee collecting pollen. "I'll show that wizard what a first-class witch I am," she cackled.

"But I need a rest before I try this out. Don't touch anything." Lobelia yawned and went to bed.

Baldrick dreamed of mice and gazed up at the moon. It looked as though it was resting on top of a tall tree.

If I climbed that tree I could reach the moon easily, he thought.

It was dark in the garden and a bit creepy. Baldrick scrambled up the tree. At last he reached the top, but the moon was now above the chimney of Lobelia's house.

Suddenly, an owl hooted and Baldrick jumped.

"Meeeoow!" he howled as he crashed through the branches, landing with a *thump* on the ground.

When he'd got his breath
back Baldrick tried
another plan.

And then another.

But Baldrick just couldn't give up the idea of those fat little moon mice.

"I know. I'll try Lobelia's new spell!" he meowed triumphantly.

He carefully measured all the ingredients into the big black cauldron. The very last thing on the list was "one drop of fresh bee sting." Baldrick wasn't sure how much one drop was but he shut his eyes and tipped up the bottle.

There was a terrible flash and a lot of smoke.

Baldrick was so frightened that his fur stood up on end. He felt very strange — not at all like himself.

"Oh no!" he squeaked. "I hope this spell wears off."

But he wasn't at all sure that it would.

Anyway, he thought more cheerfully, now I can fly to the moon with these funny little wings.

He jumped up and launched himself into the air.

The wings worked beautifully and made an odd buzzing noise.

Baldrick made a beeline for the moon. As he drew nearer to the surface he could see some creatures scurrying about. Suddenly, several of them spotted him and jumped up and down, pointing excitedly. Baldrick could see that they were mice — and they were green!

They seem quite big, he thought as he got a bit closer. They seem very big indeed. "Oh, my whiskers, they're enormice!" he wailed as he landed on the moon with a giant *thud*!

The moon mice clustered around Baldrick curiously.

"Who are you?" demanded the largest one.

"I'm Baldrick the cat," squeaked Baldrick faintly.

"A cat? Are you sure?" asked a mouse. "You don't look like a cat."

"We don't want any cats here," shrieked another.

Instantly, Baldrick was seized by strong green claws and pushed from mouse to mouse until he was quite giddy. He clung to a lump of moon rock, trembling with fear.

"I bet he'd taste delicious with a nice cheese sauce," said the largest mouse. Just then there was a *whoosh* overhead, and Lobelia swept down on her broomstick and plucked Baldrick from the middle of the mob. The mice yelled and jeered as the broomstick sped off into the night.

Lobelia grasped Baldrick by the scruff of his neck and shook him till his teeth rattled.

"I told you not to touch anything," she screeched. "You naughty, disobedient . . ."

But before she could finish, her broomstick bucked like a wild horse and plummeted toward the earth, completely out of control.

Lobelia shrieked and let go of Baldrick, who slid helter-skelter down the broomstick.

He opened his mouth to yell, but all that came out was a curious buzz. Then he remembered his wings and beat them with all his strength. At the very last moment he pulled the broomstick out of the dive and crash-landed in some bushes.

Baldrick was a hero.

The rock that he had been clutching the whole time was, of course, green cheese.

Lobelia was so pleased that she transformed him back to normal in an instant and allowed him to present the cheese to the wizard.

Baldrick was awarded the Silver Cauldron Medal (1st class) and an advanced broomstick license.

"Well, Baldrick," said Lobelia, "you certainly deserve a treat. How about chocolate-covered mice?"

"Please, Lobelia," said Baldrick shyly. "I think I'd rather have sardines."